"Readers aren't born, they're made. Desire is planted—planted by parents who work at it."

—Jim Trelease
author of *The Read Aloud Handbook*

"When I was a classroom reading teacher, I recognized the importance of good stories in making children understand that reading is more than just recognizing words. I saw that children who get excited about reading and who have ready access to books make noticeably greater gains in reading comprehension and fluency. The development of the HELLO READING™ series grows out of this experience."

—Harriet Ziefert

Harriet Ziefert lives in Maplewood, New Jersey, and has taught children from preschool age up to 11-12 year-olds. She has written numerous books for children including NICKY'S NOISY NIGHT, NICKY'S PICNIC and WHERE'S MY EASTER EGG for very young readers, also published in Puffin Books.

Jill Bennett, who adapted the text for this edition, trained as a teacher and is now in charge of a reading centre near London. She is the author of several book guides including the highly acclaimed and influential LEARNING TO READ WITH PICTURE BOOKS.

For A. M. B., who knows
good dreams come on good nights

PUFFIN BOOKS
Published by the Penguin Group
27 Wrights Lane, London W8 5TZ, England
Viking Penguin Inc., 40 West 23rd Street, New York, New York 10010, USA
Penguin Books Australia Ltd, Ringwood, Victoria, Australia
Penguin Books Canada Ltd, 2801 John Street, Markham, Ontario, Canada L3R 1B4
Penguin Books (NZ) Ltd, 182–190 Wairau Road, Auckland 10, New Zealand

Penguin Books Ltd, Registered Offices: Harmondsworth, Middlesex, England

First published in the USA in Puffin Books 1987
This edition published in Great Britain 1988

Text copyright © Harriet Ziefert, 1987, 1988
Illustrations copyright © Catherine Siracusa, 1987
All rights reserved

Text anglicized by Jill Bennett

Printed in Singapore for Harriet Ziefert, Inc.

SAY GOOD NIGHT!

Harriet Ziefert
Illustrated by Catherine Siracusa

PUFFIN BOOKS

Amanda's parents peeped round her bedroom door. "Good night," they said.

Amanda did not want
to say good night.

"Why *good*?" Amanda asked.
"What's good
about the night?"

"Well," said mum, "on a good night
you can see the moon."

Amanda saw the moon outside.
"Yes," she thought, "the moon
does look good."

"A good night means you can
hear quiet," said mum.

"And quiet is peaceful."

A soft breeze blew.
It tickled Amanda's face.

"Maybe it's blowing me
a dream," thought Amanda.

"Good dreams come on good nights," Amanda heard mum say.

"Now you *must*
go to sleep.
Good night.
Good…

night!"

"Good night.
Turn off the light please mummy,"
whispered Amanda.

"Sleep tight, sleep tight,
till morning light," said mum
as she closed the door.

It seemed no time at all till
Amanda heard mum and dad again.
"Good morning," they said.

"Why *good*?" Amanda asked.
"What's good about the morning?"

"On a good morning you can
see the sun," said dad
as he drew her curtains.

"You can smell
bacon and eggs...

and hear music
from the radio."

"Are you getting up today?"
asked dad.

"It's a good morning.
We could go to the park later."

"Breakfast's ready," called mum.
"Come on."

"All right, coming,"
said Amanda.

"Good morning!"